The Last Robot
and Other Science Fiction Poems

Jane Yolen

ISBN 978-1-8381268-1-0

Published by

Shoreline of Infinity

Edinburgh, Scotland

www.shorelineofInfinity.com

Cover illustration: Emily Simeoni
Wee robots: Becca McCall
Design: The New Curiosity Shop
Back cover photo: Jason Stemple
The glove photo: Lin Oliver

Contents

The Last Robot and other Science Fiction Poems was awarded the Elgin prize for best Chapbook in 2023. The Elgin prize is awarded by the Science Fiction & Poetry Association.

www.sfpoetry.com/el/23elgin.html

Acknowledgements

Mars Rover, Curiosity @2019 Asimov's Magazine
Ode to Cassini @2020 Asimov's Magazine
Nice Touch @2015 Asimov's Magazine
Stardust @2017 Shoreline of Infinity
Ripples in Space-Time @2018 Meat for Tea
Can SciFi Save Us? @2018 Shoreline of Infinity
Now A Ragged Breeze @2018 Shoreline of Infinity
That Rocky Ride @2019 F&SF Magazine
Robot Dreams @2018 Asimov's Magazine
Robot Love @2017 Typishly
Robot Baby ©2018 Shoreline of Infinity anthology

Planet Earth

Light

A word but not a word,
sound, but not sound,
a puff of air, a hiss of breath,
a shift of molecules
before there were molecules.

A star born before it has a name,
a garden planted with nouns,
green not yet a color and yet
surely a color, pushing up
through what will one day be called
Ground Zero.

Something is born, from the earth,
from the star, vaguely man-like,
woman-like, but a surer touch
this time. Alike and not alike.

Something flies above their heads.
"Bird," the man figure says.
"Hawk," the woman figure says.
An argument from the beginning.

Can SciFi Save Us?

No more than a single politician,
or the signing of a solitary bill.
No more than a march of a thousand, a million,
or the rise of a green sunburst.
No more than a man in a grey suit
holding a placard outside Parliament,
or a dozen protestors inside.
No more than a woman mowed down
by a Nazi on a soft morning,
nor a dozen dozen school children
slaughtered at their desks.

But a single story told enough times,
warmed in the mouths of a thousand tellers,
resurrected from a cross of Martian timber,
plowed into the dirt of a million stars
might make a difference.
Perhaps long after we are gone,
and our paper with us,
there will be alien visitors
who, in a language different from ours,
will coin a new word for SciFi,
and create tales that will erase
all our planetary scars,
setting the heavens alight again.

That Shining Word

"I know nothing in the world that has as much power as a word. Sometimes I write one, and I look at it, until it begins to shine."

—Emily Dickinson

That little shining sun,
that singularity,
that mirror to enchantment,
that faceted jewel,
that window on wonder,
that natured pearl,
that planet in nova,
that explosive caldera,
that burst of star
across the dark heavens,
falling, falling onto the page,
that perfect word.

We could power the universe with it.

Now a Ragged Breeze

Now a ragged breeze as the damp earth breathes,
a gasp, a grasp at metaphor, some over-the-top
reference to oceans or volcanoes, one cool, one hot,
both damp in a funny way. Why doesn't the poet
be specific, that terrific and terrible blend
of art and science. Ragged can be measured,
damp felt, and earth, that Gaian concept
of Lovelock's devising, colonies of microbes,
laughing at our feelings of superiority,
while they keep symbiotically marching
forward to define and refine the planet
as we stand apostrophizing sky.
Meanwhile below, the very mud seethes
with rebellions, its symbiotes making plans
to destroy our poems, insert theirs,
as their children, the lowly slime moulds,
inherit.

That Rocky Ride

"Earth is the only rock
we have to ride."
—David L. Harrison

Earth is the only rock
we have to ride now.
Its heft and hurtle
through the universe--
the only poem we know.

But our children's children
will hitch their rides
to different rocks,
sing other odes,
rope further stars.

They will ride into 'verses,
make poems
we cannot imagine,
speak metaphors,
in mouths unlike our own.

Baby Boy in Utero

"the world-shouldering monstrous "I".
—Ted Hughes

So it is, child, as you hurtle
through the black space
of your mother into the light
and into ego, that "I"
going forth before you,
monstrous erection of self,
comet-tailed combustion,
wrecking ball of the future.

And yet there in the cradle
your unsuspicious eyes closing,
a droplet of warm milk
on lips not open with demands.
How quiet the room,
how still the universe.
A moment's respite
before the world burns.

God's Carton

Egg cradle, the shell
held in angel arms,
a singularity waiting
to become a world.
No Big Bang here,
but the gentle opening
onto the fry pan
of the universe.
The only question—
will it be a watery Earth,
dry Mars,
or your basic,
everyday galactic
scramble?

There Is No Space Bar in the Universe

The universe itself is a poem.
No mistaking it for prose.
Sky, stars, planets, named
and unnamed, are more metaphor
than real, to the few who have stepped
on the moon, held moon rocks in the odd light.
Though those few have been stripped
of their common humanity
and been turned into stanzas.
Why else were the first two
named Armstrong and Buzz
clearly chosen for the branding,
such forward thinking of the space group.

Long Sight

Even from the space station
those fires can be seen,
blurring misting, smoking,
over the north of the Amazon,
the south of Australia.
It looks like fuzz, like fluff,
planetary dust
under the bed.
Only the debate,
the blame game,
can be seen
sparking through
that gray destruction.
Travelers from distant planets
will now avoid us.
"Ash" is what they will call Earth,
that burned place,
that dusty hole
in an otherwise universe
of civil-izations.

Landing

Our ship, Wander, touched down
on the third planet, its sun
brighter than ours had ever been,
trees dancing like tzitzit
on the bottom of a shawl.

Like God's Eden, the captain thought
landing near a blue sea so great
we could not see its end.
And like God's mercy, he added,
though none had been given before.

The landing party left, kissing the mezuzah,
hoping for a quiet welcome,
no other populations to greet them,
with cudgels. With guns. With knives.
With ovens.

When we left that Paradise, serpent alley,
that earth was scorched.
Our numbers halved.
A desert living in the captain's heart,
commanded us to plow once more

the paths of the infinite sky.

Outer Space

Making Furrows

We make furrows on this planet,
deep wounds with iron
the fairies have warned about.
The world bleeds green,
then rust. Autumn practices death.
When I saw oil fields in Oklahoma
twenty years ago, I knew I looked
on the face of a new Mars.
Who will now send Rover chasing
across these deserts
sending messages back
to an alien world?

Mars Rover, Curiosity

It tracks across the landscape,
one sol after another.
It may know day from night,
may know the planet
has 668 sols,
but in stubborn obeisance
to its own makers,
it marks all its anniversaries
in Earth time.

I am of that same curious metal
plodding place to place.
The sun, the moon are flags
I recognize, but planted
in my own known earth.
I count my hours
by those remembered chimes
that ring out the time
in my small town.

NASA's Hammer

That probe, that small landing,
that new hammer
hitting the atmosphere.
Such a precise angle,
an angel with singed wings,
probing below,
the hell that is Mars,
a Hades of its own,
seven minutes of terror
and then came
The Word.

So we learn,
so we parse the many heavens,
landing in seven minutes
on a place that took
the god of Mars
seven days, more or less
to create.

Titan's Lakes

Ethane and Methane went for a dip,
according to Cassini's ship.
So far from Earth, the probe slipped by,
watching with a quite human eye.

These sudden ponds, as thick as stone,
reminded us, somehow, of home,
though nine times further from the sun.
Not water blessed by anyone.

We named them lakes upon a whim,
this solid gas, where no fish swim.

Ode to Cassini

There is nothing now but echo,
faint beeps, like a dying heart.
He can feel the breath of doctors
at his bedside, hear family weeping.
The light, the light, he thinks,
as the angel in charge
of good machinery
gathers him into planetary arms.
Faithful to the end,
he sends his final discoveries home.

Ashes to Pluto

The silent pass of Trombaugh's ashes,
gift of our planet to yours,
celebrating discovery,
mountains, cliffs, a trough,
the signature of a minor god.

His handwriting on your surfaces,
remarking a probe's long tour,
punctuates the uncovering
of ground, both smooth and rough,
where no man's foot yet trod.

No prayers said, no rehashes
of ancient heresies, ours
is a planet of brotherly
hatreds, wars. We've enough
to export to your new sod.

Forgive us our sins, young earth,
as we prepare to plunder your hearth.

Ripples in space-time: A Found Poem (National Geographic)

Einstein confirmed:
stellar zombies
from the deaths of giant stars
that rotate around each other;
closer they get, the faster they spin,
collide,
eject gold and silver.
You, me,
a wedding ring,
years later, a death,
round and round.
So it goes.
So it goes.
So it goes.

Goblin Planet Blues

*"The Goblin is a newly confirmed dwarf planet that travels
to the fringes of the solar system ... it was first seen around
Halloween of 2015, according to Carnegie Science."*

Spinning its elliptic,
here out on the edge,
Goblin hugs the limits
of the missing Planet X.

Singing down the lanes
of the planetary skies,
it travels 'long the fringes
where the solar system lies.

*It's got the blues, such bad news,
its path too faint to see.
Singing on the outside
of that bad boy
E-tern-ity.*

Lonely in its wander,
dwarfed by the planet crowd,
little planet Goblin
sings its sorrow long and loud.

Maybe there are others
even smaller in the sky,
too tiny to be seen
by an eager seeker's eye.

It's got the blues, such bad news,
its path too faint to see.
Singing on the outside
of that bad boy
E-tern-ity.

An Invisible Möbius Strip

It signifies world's end,
this casual, causal loop
when you and I return
to the world where wonder
no longer exists, where story
is all we are, past is future.
Where the grandchildren play
around our graves
and no one remembers
to cut the grass between.

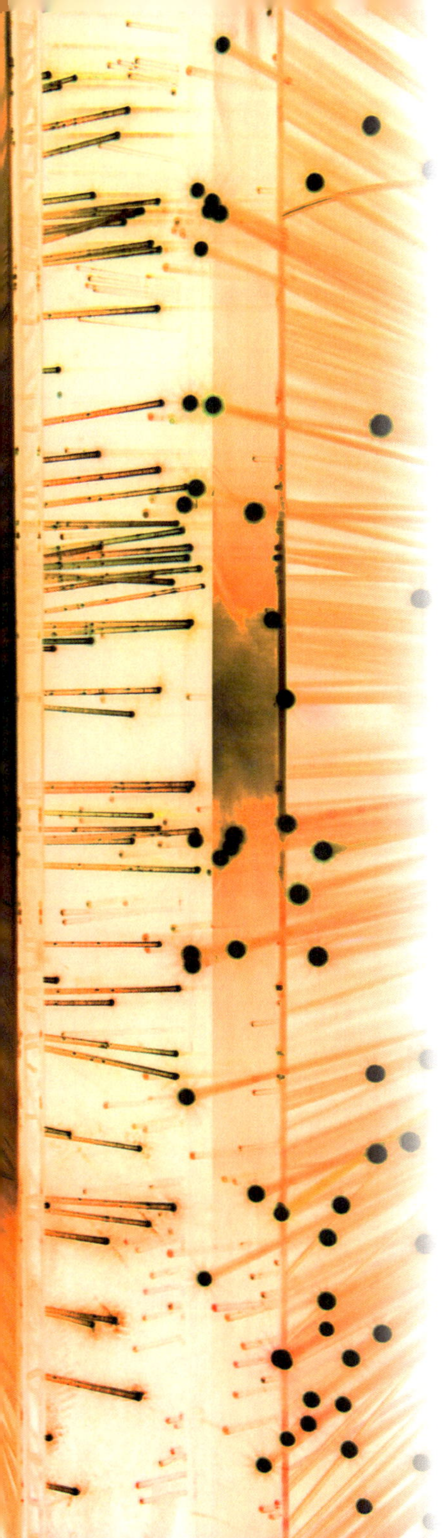

Aliens & Robots

Things Aliens Ask of Us

Why do you fight amongst yourselves
when yourselves is all you have?

Why do you frack and wrack your world
when it is your cradle and your grave?

Why do you eat the hens who give you eggs,
the sheep who give you wool?

Why do you need to go so fast from here to there
when there is much to see along the way?

Why do you not trust in story when it is you
who have dreamed your lives?

Who can be your savior when you do not
try to save yourselves?

Why do you call *us* aliens, when clearly
you are aliens on your own world?

And please explain all the manicured lawns.

Nice Touch

"The plastic bags in the ocean are a nice touch."
—Teresa Matlock

The aliens see the blue planet from afar,
come down for a closer look.
They are comfortable with the long green
corpses of golf courses,
conversant with iron cranes
pumping out life-giving oil.
They recognize the bones
of mammoth trash mountains,
dumps of old machines, batteries, wires.
Even the children searching the ruins are familiar.

The aliens turn to their hosts,
those few remaining men
and their frightened women in faded aprons.
"The plastic bags in the ocean are a nice touch,"
they say before flying off in their golden ships.
"We'll take the whole thing."

The Rebound Effect

*"The 'New world atlas of artificial night sky brightness',
published in 2016, reveals that 'around 83% of the world
population, and more than 99% of the US and European
populations live under light-polluted skies."*

God said *Let there be Light.*
He forgot the off switch.
Slowly all the stars are winking out.

Soon enough, we will look at the sky
through a man-made haze, thinking:
How beautiful the blackness,

Where once we saw the wink of planets,
the Morse of eternity,
the comforting nearness of alien stars.

1. Robot Dreams

In the machine shop, the robot dreams:
"I am the gray traveler,
the fetus of God.
Some day I will be a monument."

Who can calculate dreams
or the meaning of dreams?
Freud tried and Jung,
hanging their analytics
on the coat hook of a century
full of nightmares.

The robot was shoved
onto the conveyor belt.
From there to a delivery truck
where he thought he had arrived
on the only route to God,
side by side with the gray beauty

of his surprising peers.

2. Robot Love

It begins with a spark,
short, bright, lightning
in the command center.

There is a shock of movement,
steel lips link, lock,
a pop as one lip splits.

They fall to the floor.
Long limbs clanging
try to find a purchase.

For a moment they mimic
a thrust, hard breathing,
one cries out in ecstatic code.

Finally, there is a second spark,
a grinding noise, metal on metal,
intermittent.

3. Robot Baby

Birthed in the body shop,
polished by the nurse,
it rests in your arm
without movement or thought,
until you speak.

Its name brings life.
Excalibur,
though you will always
call it Callie.
It creaks awake.

The manual instructs:
change its oil
every few hours.
Free oilcan attached.
Use diapers for leaks.

It will never grow old,
only rust if you leave it out
too long in the rain.
It won't smoke dope,
get depressed, talk back.
It will care for you in your old age.

4. The Last Robot

The last robot on Earth
sank sullen in farmyard muck,
half-buried in a pigsty.
Even the boars, for their final meal,
turned their backs on its rusting parts

Some creatures are a mystery,
some a misery, but robots
were the perfect immigrants,
ready to work for nothing
but a bit of borrowed energy.

They lay as they lived,
outsiders even indoors,
unacknowledged laborers,
motives mistrusted,
useful until used up.

Lynched by history,
rotting by roadsides,
hated by fellow workers
and owners unlike
they never truly died.

They just cluttered the landscape
with their irony
and their iron bones,
a testament to their steadiness
and the world's bigotry.

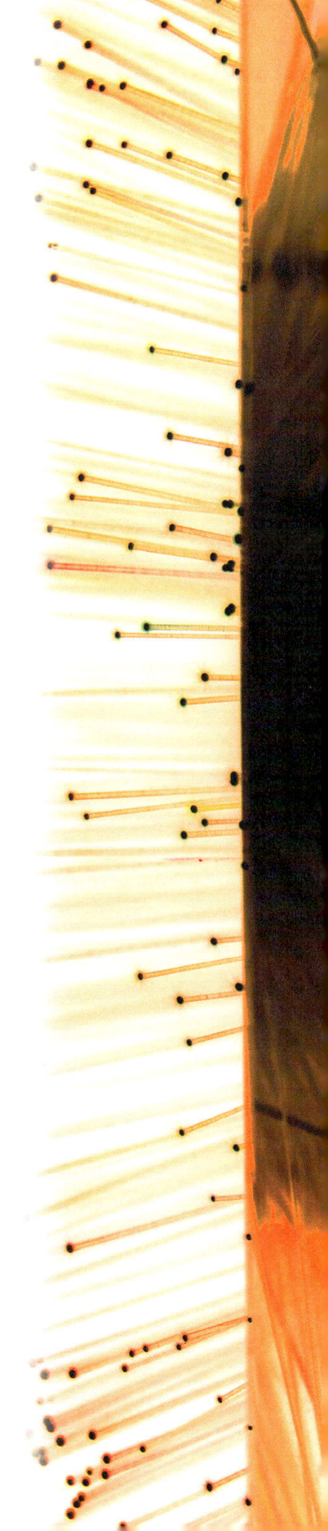

These poems were written over the course of a number of years, some sold to magazines. But it wasn't until the folks at *Shoreline of Infinity*, a wonderful award-winning Scottish sf magazine I have had poems in, asked if I would like to do a "Pamphlet" for them the idea for this book came about.

Turns out "Pamphlet" is what Americans call "Chapbook." Once that was sorted, I looked through my many poems, both published and unpublished to find the right poems for this small book. I write a poem a day for over a thousand subscribers, and have done for twelves years, so there's a lot to look through.

You, too, can get them hot off my fingertips and even before they are published anywhere, by signing up to MailChimp here:

http://eepurl.com/bs28ab

In exchange at each month's end, you promise to borrow a book of mine from your local library, re-read a book of mine you already have, or buy one. (This pamphlet counts!) As my 400th book will be published by mid 2C21, you shouldn't be at a loss for choices.

—Jane Yolen

Jane Yolen has published over 440 books, and counting. Her poems have been published in literary journals and science fiction magazines, as well as in anthologies and collections. She lives part time in Scotland, and has been the president (two years) of SFWA, the Science Fiction Writers of America.

Six colleges and universities have given her honorary doctorates for her body of work.

Jane's website is: www.janeyolen.com

Twitter: @JaneYolen